W9-DCE-941

JE – HOLIDAY

I AM THE TURKEY

story by Michele Sobel Spirn

pictures by Joy Allen

HarperCollins*Publishers*

HarperCollins®, ☞®, and I Can Read Book® are
trademarks of HarperCollins Publishers Inc.

I Am the Turkey
Library of Congress Cataloging-in-Publication Data
Spirn, Michele.
I am the turkey / story by Michele Sobel Spirn ; pictures by Joy Allen.—1st ed.
p.   cm. — (An I can read book)
Summary: Mark does not want to play the turkey in the second grade Thanksgiving play,
but then he ends up saving the day.
ISBN 0-06-053230-0 — ISBN 0-06-053231-9 (lib. bdg.)
[1. Theater—Fiction. 2. Schools—Fiction.] I. Allen, Joy, ill. II. Title. III. Series.
PZ7.S757Iae 2004
[E]—dc22
                                                                    2003019821

1   2   3   4   5   6   7   8   9   10
❖
First Edition

For Steve, as always, and Josh and Kirsten, much love and happiness. With love and thanks to my writing friends, Marthe Jocelyn and Julia Noonan
—M.S.S.

To Pack 288 of Garden Grove and Chief Shortcake!
—J.A.

THE CLASS TURKEY

I run into school.

"Slow down," says the principal.

I walk slowly to my class.

It is hard.

Today is the day we get our parts

for the Thanksgiving play.

"John, you will be a Pilgrim,"

says Ms. Willow, our teacher.

The play is a big deal.

Our parents come to see it.

I would like a good part.

A Pilgrim is a good part.

"Ron, you will be a tree,"

says Ms. Willow.

"Allie, you will be Plymouth Rock."

7

A tree? A rock?

Not me! I want a good part.

A tree does not talk.

A rock does not talk.

"Jane, you will be an Indian,"

says Ms. Willow.

An Indian is a good part.

I hope I will be an Indian

or a Pilgrim. They have a lot to say.

"Mark," says Ms. Willow.

Mark! That's me!

"You will be the turkey," she says.

The turkey?

What kind of part is that?

"The turkey is a good part,"

Ms. Willow says. "Without the turkey,

we could not have Thanksgiving."

She is right. There are many Indians.

There are many Pilgrims.

There is only one turkey.

That night at dinner my father asks,

"How was school?"

"Fine," I say. "We will put on a play

for Thanksgiving."

"Big deal," says my brother, Tim.

"A second-grade play. Ha! Ha!"

"I remember when you were
in the Thanksgiving play, Tim,"
my mother says. "You were a Pilgrim.
What part did you get, Mark?"

"A good part—the turkey," I say.

"Ha! Ha! Ha! Ha! Ha!" shouts Tim.

Milk comes out of his nose.

"You are a turkey!"

"Tim!" my mother says.

"The turkey is a good part."

I eat my meat. I eat my corn.

Tim keeps laughing.

Maybe the turkey is not

such a good part.

A DEAD DUCK

My brother tells his friends,

"Mark is the class turkey!"

They all laugh.

I find out a turkey is a fool.

No one in my class knows this.

I will not tell them.

Today we will start doing the play.

We must practice it many times

so we can be good

and remember our lines.

Our lines are what we say.

John tells how the Pilgrims

came here. He tells how hard

the first winter was.

Jane tells how the Indians
helped the Pilgrims.

I look at my lines. All I say is,

"Gobble! Gobble! Gobble!"

"Don't I say more?"

I ask Ms. Willow.

"No," says Ms. Willow.

"That is all the turkey says."

My brother tells me the real story
when we walk home from school.
"That is because you are an animal,"
he says. "And you are dead
at the end. The Pilgrims
and the Indians eat you."
"Not me!" I say. "You are just trying
to make me feel bad."
"Okay, turkey," he says. "Ask Mom."

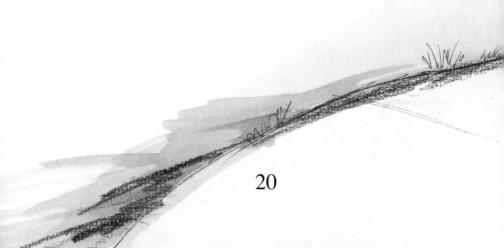

That night I ask Mom,
"Did the Indians and Pilgrims
eat turkey at Thanksgiving?"
Mom tells me about the first
Thanksgiving dinner.

Eek! I am a turkey and they eat me.

Tim is right! I am a dead duck!

23

The next day I tell Ms. Willow,

"I am sick. I cannot be in the play."

"Mark, the play is two weeks away.

I am sure you will feel better

by then," she says.

She turns away. I run after her.
"Ms. Willow, I forgot to tell you
my grandma is coming to visit,"
I say. "I will need to spend
some time with her."

"She can come to the play,"

says Ms. Willow.

That Ms. Willow!

She has an answer for everything.

She says, "You will see. The turkey

is the best part in the play.

We need you."

Yes, you need to kill me

and eat me, I think.

How did I get stuck

in such a bad part?

What can I do about it?

26

THE TURKEY SAVES THE DAY

On the day of the play,

Ms. Willow seems a little funny.

She keeps picking at our costumes.

John throws up. It is hard

to be a Pilgrim with so many lines.

Jane says she will throw up, too.

"You will be fine when you get out

on the stage," Ms. Willow says.

I know I will be fine. I have a plan.

No one who comes to see the play

will know I am the turkey.

I peek out to see who is there.

I see Mom and Dad and Tim.

Why did Tim have to come?

I think I see him pick his nose.

Good! I will tell Dad tonight

and Tim will get in trouble.

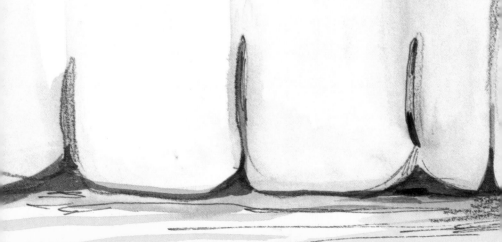

"It is time," Ms. Willow says.

"I know you will all do well."

Jane goes out. She has many lines.

She is good. People clap for her.

The other Indians go out.

"It is going fine," says Ms. Willow.

Then I go out. Now for my plan.

I bend over so I am little.

I hide behind Jane.

Jane moves.

I hide behind John.

John moves.

I hide behind Allie, the rock.

Now and then I poke my beak out

and say, "Gobble! Gobble! Gobble!"

when I have to.

People laugh.

I do not think it is that funny.

Oh, no! Allie moves.

A rock is supposed to stay still.

What kind of rock moves its feet?

I hide behind John again.

John has to talk.

He looks sick. His face is green.

It is the end of the play.

He has to say they will eat me

at the big Thanksgiving dinner.

But John does not say a word.

"Say your lines," I whisper to him.

He just looks at me

and then at the people in the seats.

The mothers all go "Oooh!"

Ms. Willow looks

like she is going to cry.

Jane and the other Indians back away.

The Pilgrims say nothing.

I think about how hard

we have worked on the play.

"Say something!" I say to Allie.

"Rocks do not talk!" she says back.

The tree has backed up

into the Pilgrims.

Someone has to do something!

I fix my wings.

I pull my beak down.

I come out from behind John.

There are a lot of people.

They are all looking at me.

"Uh, I am the turkey," I say.

I see Tim try to hide under his seat.

Mom and Dad look surprised.

"This is the end of the play.
The Pilgrims and the Indians
eat the turkey. But Thanksgiving
is for saying thanks.
And turkeys will thank you
if you do not eat them."
I bow. Everybody claps.

Ms. Willow comes over to me.

I am sure she is mad.

But she hugs me.

"Thank you, Mark," she says.

"You saved the play."

John's mother takes him home.

He still looks green.

Jane and the other Indians say,

"Mark! You were cool!"

Then my mom and dad come in.

"You were the best turkey ever!"
Mom says.

"You were great, son," Dad says.

"You were okay," says Tim.

More people come in.

They all ask, "Who was the turkey?"

I am happy to say,

"Me! I am the turkey!"